JAKE and the GIANT HAND

JAKE
and the
GIANT HAND

PHILIPPA DOWDING

Illustrations by Shawna Daigle

DUNDURN
TORONTO

Project Editor: Diane Young
Editor: Allister Thompson
Illustrator: Shawna Daigle
Interior and Cover Design: Jesse Hooper
Cover art by Shawna Daigle
Printer: Webcom

Library and Archives Canada Cataloguing in Publication

Dowding, Philippa, 1963-, author
    Jake and the giant hand : weird stories gone wrong / Philippa Dowding.

Issued in print and electronic formats.
ISBN 978-1-4597-2421-1 (pbk.).--ISBN 978-1-4597-2422-8 (pdf).--
ISBN 978-1-4597-2423-5 (epub)

    I. Title.

PS8607.O9874J35 2014   jC813'.6   C2013-908378-2
                                            C2013-908379-0

1   2   3   4   5   18   17   16   15   14

We acknowledge the support of the **Canada Council for the Arts** and the **Ontario Arts Council** for our publishing program. We also acknowledge the financial support of the **Government of Canada** through the **Canada Book Fund** and **Livres Canada Books**, and the **Government of Ontario** through the **Ontario Book Publishing Tax Credit** and the **Ontario Media Development Corporation**.

The author would like to thank the Writers' Reserve Program of the Ontario Arts Council for their support.

VISIT US AT
Dundurn.com | @dundurnpress | Facebook.com/dundurnpress | Pinterest.com/dundurnpress

Dundurn
3 Church Street, Suite 500
Toronto, Ontario, Canada
M5E 1M2

MIX
Paper from
responsible sources
FSC® C004071

For Ben, the king of weird stories

THIS PART IS
(MOSTLY) TRUE

You should know, before you even start this book, that it's a little scary. And parts of it are even a bit sad. I wish I could make the story less scary and sad, but this is the way I heard it, so I really have no choice.

It starts like this:

A long time ago, a little old lady disappeared.

She lived on a farm around here, then her husband died and her children moved away, and she took to wandering. One moonlit summer night, she just vanished. Some say she wandered into the fields and no one ever found her. (This is definitely the sad part). Others say she went to live at her brother's farm in another county, and still others say she joined the circus and lived out her days in warmth and comfort.

People had lots of ideas about what happened to her. Whatever the case, one day her son came to visit and found the house empty and dark. The back door was banging in the wind. People looked for months and years, but they never found her.

Do you want to know what I think? I think she wandered into the swamp. Once you go in … you sometimes never come out.

Here's the scary part. A little while after she vanished, people started to hear … noises coming from the swamp. Howls, cries, weird shrieking. Right around then, some say a face began to appear in windows at night and scared perfectly nice people half to death.

Some say it was her face. The little old lady who disappeared.

You don't have to believe this story. But just because things are odd or a little strange or unbelievable doesn't always make them untrue. Truth is an odd thing; one person's truth can be another person's lie. That's the most important thing to remember about this story: sometimes things that seem like lies are actually true. And sometimes you never can tell.

That's the spookiest thing of all.

CHAPTER 1

DIS-*GUS*-TING

Jake hung on. It wasn't easy.

The old pickup truck almost veered off the winding gravel road, and Jake bumped up and down on the front seat. His teeth chattered.

"Sorry, Jake," his grandpa grunted. "That fly was BIG!"

His grandpa got the truck back on the road, and Jake settled down in the front seat again. He'd be at his grandpa's farm soon.

"Did I ever tell you about the time I hunted the biggest spider in the world, Jake?" his grandpa said after a minute.

Oh, no. Jake could feel a grandpa story coming. An *exaggeration.* Or more often, a huge, impossible lie. The thing you have to know about Jake's grandpa is he told stories. Too many stories.

"No, Grandpa. You haven't told me that one. Maybe some other time? I'm kind of tired right now." Jake leaned against the door of the pickup and tried to look like he was going to sleep.

Which was fine. Until Gus tried to lick Jake's face.

What you have to know about Gus is that he smelled. Awful. Not only was he a giant, slobbering hound dog, he also wanted to lick everything.

Gus looked sad all the time, with big floppy ears and droopy eyes and a huge, panting tongue. Jake had seen that tongue-of-death lick a dead, smelly rabbit plus lots of other gross things that a tongue has no business being near. Like garbage and horse poo.

Jake wasn't too interested in having it touch his face.

"Move over, you smelly dog!" Jake gave the old hound a shove down the seat. The dog wasn't used to two people in the front seat of the truck. Whenever he went anywhere with Jake's grandpa, he pretty much had it to himself.

Except when Jake came to visit for two weeks every summer.

Jake looked out the window. It was dark out there in the fields and trees. Every once in a while, he could see a kitchen far back in a field, with a light on. Someone was having dinner in a farmhouse. But everything else was black, much darker than in the city, where Jake lived with his mom.

It was a little spooky, all those dark trees, all the empty black fields.

Jake fiddled with the old radio, but he couldn't find a station. Gus breathed in his face, so he squirmed away and looked out the window again. His grandpa was silent, staring straight ahead. Jake couldn't stand the darkness and the silence any longer.

"So, Grandpa, what are we going to do for the next two weeks?"

"Digging. This year we're building a shed," his grandpa answered with a grunt. He leaned over the steering wheel.

Shed. That was a new one. Jake was going to have to swing a hammer. Last year it was painting the barn red.

Maybe it won't be so bad. I'll build some muscles at least.

Then Jake recognized a turn in the dirt road. They were getting closer to his grandpa's farm. He looked through the darkness and could make out the trees in the distance that stood near the ... swamp.

Don't think about the swamp! Don't think about Kate Cuthbert's creepy ghost stories either....

Too late. Kate's voice from last summer popped into Jake's head.

"... a long time ago, a little old lady disappeared. She lived on a farm around here, then her husband died and her children moved away and she took to wandering...."

Jake gulped.

Think about something else!

They pulled into the driveway of Grandpa's old farmhouse. Gus bounded over Jake and out the truck door, then the smelly old dog ran to the back of the house.

It was a small farmhouse with a white front door and apple trees all around. Jake could smell the late-summer apples, even if he couldn't see them very well in the dark. The farm had been in the McGregor family for three generations, over a hundred years. His grandpa, his great-grandpa, and his great-great-grandpa had all lived there. It was a family homestead.

Jake grabbed his bag from the pickup and followed his grandpa around to the kitchen door at the back. As long as he had been coming to visit his grandpa, they had never used the front door. No one ever did.

Beside the back door was a water pump with a horse head carved out of the top. Jake ran his hand over the smooth old wood of the horse's head. It was hand-made by a soldier who was going off to the First World War. It was an interesting water pump, definitely one of a kind.

Jake walked past the horse-head pump, then past the barn that held Maggie, the real horse. She wasn't for riding anymore, but you could hook her up to a little cart, and she'd pull you to town to get ice cream.

Behind the house was a giant field with nothing growing in it except grass for the neighbour's cows. It smelled sweet, though.

Jake clomped upstairs to his room at the top of the house and dropped his backpack on the lumpy old bed. His grandpa had opened the window to air out the room. A night-time breeze that smelled like grass and sunshine blew the curtains a little. He walked over to shut the window. The swamp was back there, way back in the woods. Jake suddenly felt the hair on the back of his neck stand up.

No. Don't think about the swamp!

He forced himself to look down at Gus digging in the dirt instead. The kitchen light shone on him, and Jake could see the hound sniffing at something. Then the dog threw back his head and howled.

Crazy dog. What could be so interesting in the dirt?

Jake looked closer. Gus was eating something. It looked like a ... fly? But no fly could be *that* big. It was the size of a bat. And it was *buzzing*.

Gus chomped whatever it was in half then ate it in two gulps. Gone. Then he looked up at Jake in the window and wagged his tail. He licked his paws with the tongue-of-death.

Jake yelled out the window at the old dog. "That's disgusting! Your name is in the word disgusting, did you know that? Dis-GUS-ting. That's what you are!"

A huge fly buzzed in through the window and right into Jake's face. Its enormous wings brushed his mouth.

"EW! Gross!" Jake swatted the big fly away. It smashed into the window then buzzed lazily back outside. It was the biggest fly he had ever seen.

Weirdly big.

Jake said goodnight to his grandpa, brushed his teeth, and got into his pyjamas. But not before he made sure the window was closed and latched. He took a quick look out at the darkness ... *swamp!* ... and drew the curtains, too.

CHAPTER 2

COLD ROOMS

The next morning Jake unpacked, then took the curving wooden stairs down to the kitchen two at a time.

His grandpa was staring at the window. A big fly buzzed against the glass. Sure were a lot more flies around here than Jake remembered. Big, gross flies.

"Can I go see my friends now, Grandpa?"

"Sure," his grandpa said. "But we're having spaghetti for lunch. Please go down to the basement and grab me a can of sauce before you go. First cold room on the left. Tomorrow it's your turn to cook."

"Yeah, sure, hot dogs tomorrow!" Jake said. Whenever he came to visit, they took turns cooking. One day it was Grandpa's turn to cook, the next day it was Jake's turn. Luckily his grandpa wasn't a fussy eater, because they ate a *lot* of hot dogs when Jake was around. It was basically the only thing he knew how to cook.

That and toast.

Jake started down the steep wooden stairs in the dark, gripping the handrail. The light switch was at the bottom of the stairs. Electricity was added long after the farmhouse was built, and that's where the switch ended up. His grandpa never changed it, even though he probably should have. It wasn't exactly safe going down those steep, slippery old stairs in the dark.

Once upon a time, you would have had to go into the farmhouse basement by candlelight.

The thought made Jake's neck prickle. The basement was pitch black and smelled like musty, spidery corners and rotting leaves. Plus it was cold and damp. When he was little he had refused to go down there at all without his grandpa or grandma.

Jake snapped on the light. The couch and TV were down there, and the weird little "cold rooms." They were small rooms all around the outside of the farmhouse basement wall. They were cold and damp, because they were basically outside the house, underground.

In the days before refrigerators, people kept food like cheese and eggs in the cold rooms, but now most of the rooms were empty. A few held Grandpa's extra farm tools, and a few were locked. The first one on the left was the only one that was used all the time, and it had shelves and shelves of sauces and beans and soup and food in cans.

All those tiny, dark, locked rooms would be a great place to hide someone …

… or some*thing*. Jake shivered a little.

But he was twelve now. He wasn't going to let a dark, creepy, musty basement filled with locked little rooms bother him.

Jake walked into the first cold room on the left and scanned the shelves for spaghetti sauce. He grabbed a can and ran back up the old stairs into the kitchen.

"Bye, Grandpa, see you for lunch!" he called. He ran out the front door and into the barn. His old green bicycle was leaning against the wall. He'd been riding it since he was eight. Every year his grandpa raised the seat and the handlebars a little more and oiled it up for his visit.

Jake took a few moments to say hello to Maggie and to stroke the horse's soft nose. The old horse nodded like she remembered him from all the summers before. Then he swung his leg over the bike. It was almost too small.

"Bye, Maggie! See you soon!"

He rode off down the lane with his knees almost touching his chin, whistling as loud as he could, weaving across the gravel. It was late morning and soft sunshine filtered through the leaves. The lane was lined by big oak trees, and there were meadows on both sides with wandering cows. It smelled great, like mown grass and sweet clover and fresh air forever. It couldn't be more different from the apartment block in the city where Jake lived. That didn't smell like anything except car exhaust, garbage, and gum.

Jake rode to the Cuthberts' house, the next farmhouse down the lane. Chris and Kate Cuthbert were twins, and Jake had been friends with them since he was little. They were two years older than Jake, and they got a little bigger each year, but nothing much else ever changed about them.

The twins were out front helping their dad load a cow into a trailer. They saw Jake and ran over. Chris smiled and shook Jake's hand. Kate grabbed Jake's handlebars and slapped him on the shoulder.

Kate grinned. "Hey, Jake! Wow, that bike is *way* too small for you this year."

Kate had long, dark hair and freckles. Chris was blond and tall. For twins, they couldn't look more different. They didn't act much alike, either.

"Hey, come see this, Jake!" Kate led the way to the back of the barn. "Dad got it for us for our birthday last month."

The twins took Jake around the barn and showed him their gift: a bright blue mini-bike with silver wings painted on it. It reminded Jake of a giant fly.

Two cool skull helmets were on the seat.

"Wanna ride?" Kate grinned.

Jake grabbed a helmet and strapped it on. Kate climbed onto the seat ahead of him, strapped on her own helmet, then shouted, "Hold on!" over her shoulder. She revved the whiny engine, and they tore out of the yard and into the open field.

Jake did hold on. For dear life. They flew over rocks and through the creek bed as mud and sticks and pebbles went spinning off behind them. Then Kate veered into the woods and along a special path their dad had made for them. Jake was dizzy as trees sped past them, too fast to see. They roared back onto the field and Jake couldn't believe how small the twins' house suddenly was from the edge of the forest.

Kate idled the engine and pointed into the woods. "We built a cabin back there," she yelled. "Do you want to sleep over in it tonight? We can tell ghost stories like last year." Her voice got a little quiet and creepy.

... *a long time ago, a little old lady disappeared....*

Jake looked into the deep green woods and gulped. "Yeah, I guess," he shouted back.

A huge fly buzzed right into his face. He brushed it away.

Don't think about the swamp.... And where are all these disGUSting flies coming from?

CHAPTER 3

THIS TOWN IS WEIRD

Kate kicked the little motorcycle into gear. They were back at the twins' house in a couple of minutes.

"Wow, that was fast," breathed Jake, taking off his helmet and spitting out grass. Chris was waiting for them. He looked worried.

"Kate drives like a maniac. Next time, let *me* take you for a ride."

Kate laughed. "Don't let *Chris* take you for a ride, you'd fall asleep. He drives like a little old lady!"

Chris ignored her. "Do you want to sleep over in the cabin tonight, Jake?"

Jake nodded very slowly, but looked away. "Yeah. Kate already asked."

"Okay, see you back here at eight o'clock. Oh, bring a sleeping bag and a flashlight," Chris said, always the sensible one.

Jake didn't whistle as he rode home. Instead, he kept looking over his shoulder into the woods. For the first time ever, he wasn't sure he wanted to sleep over at the Cuthberts'. Or in a cabin in the woods. Kate Cuthbert's ghost stories had a nasty habit of staying in your head and keeping you up at night, for years.

... a long time ago, a little old lady disappeared....

Jake shuddered and dropped his bike in the barn. He stopped to say hello to Maggie, then went into the farmhouse kitchen. The house smelled like spaghetti sauce.

"I'm starving, Grandpa! Let's eat!" Jake yelled too cheerfully. He set the table, and he and his grandpa ate their lunch.

His grandpa pushed his plate away and sighed. He picked at his teeth with a toothpick and looked out the kitchen window at the afternoon sun on the fields. Jake pushed his spaghetti around on his plate. He really wasn't very hungry.

"Grandpa?" he finally said.

"Uh-huh?"

Jake was silent. A cabin in the woods. Kate's creepy stories. *Swamp!*

"Cat got your tongue there, Jake?" his grandpa teased. Jake squirmed a little. He hated when his grandpa teased him.

"No. I just wanted to know if I can sleep over ... at the Cuthberts' tonight? They have a new cabin. In the woods." Jake spoke fast, all the words jumbled together. His grandpa heard him, though, and nodded.

"Did I ever tell you about the time I slept in a cabin at the edge of the world?" His grandpa grinned and winked at him.

Jake felt a story coming on, a crazy grandpa story. Jake's grandpa told stories A LOT. Which is another way of saying he told lies.

They were interesting lies, though. And sometimes he'd surprise you by actually telling you the truth. Like the time he told Jake he once worked as a lion-tamer. Jake refused to believe it until he asked his mom.

She said, "Actually, Jake, it's true. Your grandpa *did* work one summer as a lion-tamer in a travelling circus when he was a teenager. Although I'm not sure how much taming was involved. Grandma always said the lion was really old and had arthritis and no teeth or claws."

So you never really knew for sure what was true and what wasn't when it came to Jake's grandpa.

Right now, Jake didn't have time for one of his grandpa's stories. He didn't want to be teased. He was twelve now, and suddenly he just wanted permission to go to sleep at his friends' house. Was that too much to ask? If he didn't hang out with Chris and Kate, there wasn't going to be much else to do for the next two weeks.

"No, Grandpa. I haven't heard that one, about the cabin at the end of the world. Can you tell me another time? I really just want to go. Chris and Kate want me to sleep over in their new cabin in the woods tonight. Is that okay?"

His grandpa looked a little disappointed but grew serious. He leaned back further in his chair and stared at his grandson before answering.

"Didn't those two kids scare the bejeebers out of you last year with that story about poor Edwina Fingles getting lost in the swamp? They are two years older than you, you know."

Jake was surprised that his grandpa knew how scared he was last year. He wondered if he seemed that scared now.

... a long time ago, a little old lady disappeared....

Jake sat up straighter and forced himself not to think about being scared by Kate's stories. They were just stories, it was fun to hang out with the twins, and he was a year older now.

This year was going to be different.

His pride was a little hurt, which is why he said what he said next.

"No, I wasn't scared of some dumb ghost story about a ... swamp creature that lived in the woods around here. A bat *did* bang into the window right when Kate got to the part where the creature ... the little old lady ... Edwina Fingles ... wandered around knocking on windows. That freaked us all out a little. But I'm a year older now, Grandpa. It's fine."

His grandpa stopped smiling. He just looked at Jake for a while then said, "A bat, huh? Sure, you can sleep in the cabin with the twins tonight. But this town is a little weird, Jake, just keep that in mind."

Then his grandpa went for his nap, and Jake spent the rest of the afternoon bravely playing ball with Gus. It was brave because Gus kept trying to eat the ball, and the tongue-of-death was everywhere.

But it was also brave because big, juicy flies kept smacking into Jake. They'd come out of nowhere with a huge buzz then slam into the side of his head or into his back. Even Gus stopped trying to bite them after a while and hid when he saw one coming.

Eventually, Jake had to give up and go inside to watch TV in the basement with the creepy cold rooms.

Which was *braver still*.

CHAPTER 4

G-R-A-B

Jake was riding down the laneway. His grandpa hadn't let him go until after dinner was over (hot dogs) and they had done the dishes, but finally it was time. Jake had a sleeping bag and extra clothes in his backpack, plus his grandpa gave him a flashlight, a box of cookies, and three cans of pop. For the long night ahead, he said.

His grandpa also made him take Gus along, which was a little weird since Gus never went anywhere without Grandpa. Jake had Gus on a leash and was leading him beside the bike. The old hound dog wasn't happy about going with Jake. It took a lot of coaxing with dog treats. Jake had a pocketful for later.

He and Gus pulled up into the Cuthberts' front yard. He leaned his bike against the fence and led Gus along. He knocked on the front door and jumped back when it opened right away. Mr. Cuthbert said, "They're already back there, Jake. I'll let them know to meet you halfway. Just start walking back through the field to the woods."

Then he shut the door.

Jake nodded. "Okay," he said to the closed door. He and Gus started walking slowly through the field behind the house.

It was getting dark, and it was really quiet. Jake couldn't hear anything. In the city, there was always something to hear: trucks grinding their gears, emergency sirens, kids laughing down the street, people shouting, dogs barking. But it wasn't like that here. It was quiet, too quiet. There weren't any birds singing, or any cows mooing, or any sign of life at all. He looked across the field and saw the light shining in his grandpa's kitchen window.

It made him feel a little better. The stars were coming out, and a quarter moon was rising. It was a beautiful night. He and Gus made it to the edge of the forest, then he stopped to wait.

He couldn't see a pathway into the woods. Mr. Cuthbert had said he would let the twins know to come and get him, but he didn't say *how* he was going to do that. Jake had no idea where the cabin was, so he'd have to trust that they'd come to find him.

It was really dark now. Jake sat on his sleeping bag and rubbed Gus's head. The old dog smelled terrible, but suddenly Jake was kind of glad Gus was there.

Then there *were* tiny noises in the bushes.

The grass *did* sway in the moonlight.

The air *was* alive with the smell of damp, rotting leaves.

There was NO WAY Jake was going to think about the swamp ...

"... AAAHHH!"

A *hand* had grabbed Jake's shoulder!

CHAPTER 5

THE GIANT HAND

It took Jake a while to stop shrieking. It took a longer while for his heart to stop pounding out of his ribcage, too. Kate was laughing, but he didn't think it was all that funny. He tried not to look mad.

"Man! You guys are easy to sneak up on! What's that old hound dog for, anyway! He didn't even smell me. You look scared!" Kate said.

Gus wagged his tail and licked Kate's hand. Stupid dog didn't even bark. Jake felt dumb. But he had to admit, he was happy to see Kate, even if she *had* scared him half to death. She turned on a flashlight then led him along a winding, dark path through the woods to the cabin. No one would ever be able to find it if they didn't know *exactly* where to look.

Jake gulped.

As they got near, he could see it was a nice cabin, though. It looked really cozy, with warm light spilling out into the dark night.

Suddenly, a creepy white grin leapt out at Jake. He gasped and hesitated. Leaning up against the cabin wall under the window was a huge white skull and antlers. It stared and grinned at Jake in the light from the window.

Kate pointed at it. "That's a moose skull and antlers Chris and I found back in the swamp last year. Dad is going to help us hang it above the door. It's really old, since it's bleached so white from the sun."

A skull?

Jake looked closely at the dried bone: so white and strong. He knocked on it. It sounded solid.

"Yeah, that'll look great above the door," he said, trying to sound impressed. The moose skull was a little gruesome, and it came from the *swamp*. The huge skull stared at him with empty eye sockets. Jake pretended to like it, but he hoped it didn't give him nightmares.

It had been alive once. How did the moose die? Did it get stuck in the swampy water and dragged down into the muck? Jake made himself stop thinking about the moose skull.

Poor moose!

He had to think about something else. The cabin had patterned wood all around it, which made it look like something out of a storybook. He tried to change the subject.

"That looks nice," Jake said, pointing at the patterned wood. Kate stopped on the step. "Oh yeah, it took Dad and me and Chris ages to cut it all. That was the hardest part. Dad said he had a cabin just like this when he was a kid. He calls it 'gingerbread.'"

"A … *gingerbread* house in the woods?" Jake said, a little weakly.

Kate laughed. "Yeah, I guess you could say that. We've got Hansel and Gretel inside!"

Jake made a laughing noise, but he didn't feel like laughing.

Kate opened the cabin door. The lights were on, and Chris was making something in a frying pan on a stove.

It smelled fantastic.

"S'mores!" Chris said happily. "Do you like chocolate and marshmallows and graham crackers, Jake?"

Jake smiled. At least the inside of the cabin seemed normal.

"Yeah, of course." He dropped his backpack in a corner, and Gus flopped down and fell asleep.

They ate delicious s'mores until Kate finally said it was time for ghost stories and unrolled her sleeping bag in the middle of the floor. Chris and Jake unrolled their sleeping bags, too.

"Where are the beds?" Jake asked.

"We don't have any beds or anything in here yet, we just sleep on the floor," Chris said. "We'll get furniture and beds and a table and stuff one day, I guess." He shrugged.

Kate grinned and added, "It's perfect for telling ghost stories, though!"

Gus rolled over but didn't wake up. He was probably lost in hound-dog dreams about chasing rabbits. His whole body twitched. Jake wished he were far away in dreamland somewhere, too.

Kate switched off the overhead light and brought out a flashlight. Chris turned off the little stove and the cabin got dark and spooky. The flashlight beam bounced off the walls, making everything look jiggly and strange. Jake sat on his sleeping bag and pulled out his own flashlight. He was glad … so very glad … that his grandpa made him take it along.

"Okay, this is a true story … it happened around here a long time ago."

"Is it about the little old lady and the swamp?" Jake blurted out. He really didn't mean to, but he couldn't help it.

Kate shook her head. "No, that's *last* year's story. Besides, everyone knows *that* story isn't real. This story I'm going to tell you IS real. It's about a farmer's field … and a giant hand," she began.

Chris lay on his sleeping bag with his hands under his head, looking at the ceiling. He guffawed. "Oh, not this story Kate, it's stupid! It's not even scary!"

Kate scowled at her brother. "It's true, Chris. And it's *creepy*. Now quiet and listen."

Jake was more interested in creepy than scary. His mind started to wander to swamp creatures, and he sat up straighter.

Kate went on in a quiet, whispery voice. "Okay. This is a true story, and it happened a long time ago right around here. One day a farmer and his son woke up to a terrible sound. It got louder and louder. They were too scared to get out of bed, it was so loud. It was like chainsaws, like a million worker bees, like a sound that you recognized but didn't want to be real. They tiptoed downstairs … the noise was coming from the kitchen! Slowly they opened the creaky old kitchen door … and peeked inside...."

Kate's flashlight flickered on her face as she spoke. Her eyes looked dark, her forehead huge and weird. Jake clutched his own flashlight, his eyes wide.

"Do you know what was in there? The *grossest* thing you can imagine," she breathed.

"Nnn … n-no. What was it?" Jake whispered.

"FLIES! Millions of huge, HUGE flies! They came in the open window. There were so many flies, the farmer and his son couldn't open their eyes, and they couldn't open their mouths to scream for help. The flies were everywhere, buzzing in their faces, sticking to their skin, crawling in their ears, clinging to the ceilings and walls."

"Gross," Jake said in a tiny squeak.

Flies?

"Yeah, and these weren't any ordinary flies, either. These were giant flies, like butterflies, like bats, like birds! WAY TOO BIG to be normal. So the farmer and his son took one look and slammed the kitchen door and ran outside. Screaming. The air was filled with buzzing like a million chainsaws, it was driving them crazy. But then they saw something even grosser...." Kate paused. She grinned and the light from the flashlight bounced off her teeth and forehead, making her eyes look huge and empty, like sockets. She looked like a skull come to life.

Jake tried not to think of the horrible moose skull propped up against the wall outside. He stared at her, barely breathing. His flashlight started to shake, and the light on the ceiling trembled like it was crawling ... with flies! He couldn't sit still.

Chris was lying on his sleeping bag, looking up at the wooden beams in the ceiling. He seemed bored.

Kate went on, dropping her voice really low. "They *smelled* it first. A terrible reek that made them gag. They put their sleeves over their noses and mouths." She lifted her arm and covered her nose.

"Then they *heard* the buzzards and crows, screaming and shrieking." Kate covered her ears, like a loud noise was hurting her.

"Then they *saw* it. Up in the field. The grossest, most disgusting thing you could ever imagine ... a huge lump of rotten goo. Just a giant hill of blood and gross gooey stuff. *What was it?*" Kate demanded.

Jake shook his head, his mouth open. He couldn't speak.

"The thing was rotten ... *dead*. And it was *swarming* with the biggest flies you've ever seen! The farmer and his son covered their noses with scarves, their eyes with goggles, and their heads with straw hats. Then they rode their tractor into the field. Closer and closer they got ... to the *thing*. Then they saw it...."

Kate paused and looked at Jake. He was barely breathing. The cabin was so dark, and quiet, and way out in the middle of the woods. No one was around to help. Anything could be out there ... waiting. Any enormous, dead, gross thing.

Jake gulped, his heart pounding. "What was it?" he whispered, clutching his flashlight to his chest.

"It was a *giant … corpse … hand*…." Kate whispered back, her voice cracking. "With five HUGE fingers, each as big as a tractor. It was just like a normal human hand, except it was as big as a shed. And it was rotting, and it reeked. White bones stuck out where the flesh was missing. The buzzards and crows circled and dive-bombed … but the worst part …"

"Yeah?" Jake breathed. *What could possibly be worse than a huge rotting hand crawling with giant flies?*

"It was wearing a *WEDDING RING*!" Chris shouted in a loud voice that made Jake and Kate jump. Gus woke up and whined, wagging his tail down low, and slipped over to Jake's side. Jake put his arm over Gus's back and stroked him. He was glad to have something to hug; it hid his shaking hands.

"A *wedding ring*? That's *so* creepy!" Jake said.

Chris ignored him and carried on in his loud, out-of-place voice. "Yes, a wedding ring. It was huge and it had a message engraved in it. It said, '*To M Love L on Our Wedding Day.*'"

Jake looked at Kate, who nodded. "That's what they say," she said solemnly.

It was the single weirdest thing Jake had ever heard.

A wedding ring?

Jake was about to ask how anyone knew what was engraved on the ring, but Chris interrupted him. He was laughing and shaking his head.

"No one believes that story, Kate. A, because it's impossible, and B, because it's just stupid. Where did the giant hand come from? How did it end up in the field? What was it doing there? And where's the proof? Honestly, you think up the stupidest things, I don't even know where you get this stuff."

Kate looked hurt. "I'm not making it up! Mrs. Cody, the librarian in town, told us about it at a ghost walk last year. It really happened, like a hundred years ago or something, right around here. Sometimes weird things just happen. There doesn't always have to be a reason, or proof, for something weird to happen. It was just some strange thing that happened to a farmer around here, that's all."

"Okay, what happened to the hand then? If there was a giant hand in some farmer's field, where did the bones go? Why didn't all the news stations in the world come to town to report it? How come *you're* the one telling me about it, and not some important historian?" Jake was glad that Chris was making so much sense. It was a creepy story, but if you thought about it, it didn't seem *real*. It was pretty far-fetched.

Kate shrugged as she spoke. "Well, Mrs. Cody said that the farmer and his son dug a huge hole and buried the thing. They just buried the horrible hand right there, in the field. No one made a big deal about it because they buried it and kept it quiet. And when anyone asked, they denied it ever existed."

Then two really weird things happened. Gus started barking, which made Jake and Kate almost jump out of their skins.

Then *something* knocked on the window.

IT WAS A GIANT, ROTTING HAND!

CHAPTER 6

SPOOOOOKY ENOUGH
FOR YOU?

The hand rapped on the glass.

Jake and Kate looked at each other. Jake didn't make a sound. He couldn't.

But the next second Gus bounded over to the door, wagging his tail. Then Jake heard his grandpa's voice. "Jake! You in there? Open up, it's your grandpa! Hush there, Gus! Hush off barking."

Chris ran to the door and opened it, since Jake and Kate were frozen to the spot on their sleeping bags. "Mr. McGregor. Hi. We were just telling ghost stories. Actually, my sister was just telling us this really boring story about some old rotting hand in a field or something that no one believes because it's just plain dumb. Would you like to come in for some s'mores?" Chris was polite, opening the door wide.

Jake's grandpa leaned against the door frame with one hand on his knee. He shook his head. "No. No thanks, Christopher. I just came to remind Jake that he has swimming lessons early in the morning, so not to stay up too late."

He looked Jake right in the eye. "Your mom just phoned to remind me, so we better not forget. I'll be by in the morning real early to get you, Jake. Around eight o'clock, so don't stay up too late."

"Yeah, thanks Grandpa, I ... I forgot too," Jake stammered. He totally forgot that his mom had signed him up for swimming lessons at the local pool. He didn't want the lessons, but she had insisted. She didn't want him doing nothing around the farm for two weeks. Guess she didn't know about the shed he was supposed to build.

Jake thought that if his grandpa asked him if he wanted to go home, right then and there, he would have said yes. But his grandpa didn't ask.

"Okay then, see you tomorrow morning. Sleep tight. Here, Gus," his grandpa called to the dog. Jake wished Gus could stay behind, but the dog seemed happy to go home with his master.

Chris shut the door, then turned back to Jake and Kate with a wicked grin.

"*Sp-ooooo-ky* enough for you?" Chris made a ghostly "wooo" sound when he said "spooky."

"Almost like your grandpa turned up on purpose, wouldn't you say, Jake? Like he didn't like us talking about the 'giant hand' or something. You guys were so scared!" Chris laughed and shook his head. Jake and Kate just stared at him.

"Well, a *hand* rapped on the glass, Chris, right after I told the story! Of course we were scared!" Kate said. She sounded a little upset.

"What a lame story, Kate, honestly. You are so lame." Chris laughed quietly to himself and started making a second batch of s'mores.

Kate whispered to Jake, "Chris has no imagination sometimes. He reads too many history books, or mysteries where everything has a reasonable explanation at the end. I think the giant hand happened. It might have. Weird things do happen, you know?"

"Yeah, okay, whatever Kate. I should get some sleep," Jake said. He lay down on his sleeping bag and put his arm over his eyes. Like he was *ever* going to get to sleep.

"Hey, you guys want to play with the Ouija board?" Chris asked from the stove.

"NO!" Jake and Kate shouted back.

"No, let's play cards," Kate answered in a forced, overly normal voice. "Jake's got to go to sleep, anyway. He's getting up early, remember?"

Chris grunted and turned back to the stove.

"Who wants s'mores?" was the last thing Jake heard before he fell asleep.

If you can call it sleep when you toss and turn all night, having nightmares about giant rotting corpse hands. And flies.

Lots and lots of flies.

CHAPTER 7

MONSTER FLY

Jake hardly slept. He had three strange dreams.

First he dreamed he was an enormous fly, buzzing around his grandpa's head.

He wanted his grandpa to know it was him, but every time he buzzed around the old man, his grandpa tried to swat him. When his grandpa finally pulled out a can of bug spray, Jake woke up yelling.

Chris told him to go back to sleep. Jake tossed and turned.

Dream number two was about giant, buzzy fly-men visiting his grandpa's farmhouse. They were sitting in his grandma's best armchairs with their hairy, sticky legs crossed, drinking tea, making polite, buzzy conversation.

"Zzzzzoooo ... Jake ... zzzzzzz ... how do you ... zzzzz ... like the weather in zzzese parts?"

That was strange enough, but then Jake had the worst dream of all. He was a tiny person stuck to Gus's back. He hung on for dear life as Gus tore through the field, running from something. Whatever was chasing them made a loud, angry buzzing noise. The buzzing kept getting closer, and closer. He and Gus couldn't get away ... until Jake woke up sweating and shaking.

Jake was glad when he could see the sky grow lighter. He sat up in his sleeping bag and rubbed his eyes. Chris and Kate were still asleep, and Kate was snoring. Chris was spread across his sleeping bag with chocolate smeared on his face. The little kitchen was a mess, with chocolate and graham crackers and marshmallows spilled everywhere. Plus, as the sun warmed it up, the place was starting to smell like Chris's sweaty gym socks.

"Ew. Glad I'm leaving," Jake said quietly to himself.

He stretched and scratched his head. He yawned a few times. As he was reaching for his shoes, he froze. A huge fly was buzzing against the window. It was banging against the glass again and again, trying to get out.

A fly? That thing was in here all night?

It was the biggest fly he'd ever seen. It was the size of a much bigger bug. A dragon-fly maybe.

Jake tiptoed across the cabin. He picked up his running shoe and edged his way closer to the monster fly. He raised his hand, took aim, and whipped the shoe.

Direct hit!

The huge fly fell to the floor, dead. It actually made a little thud when it landed. Jake cautiously drew closer. Big, big monster fly. Each leg looked like a small finger, the wings were as big as his hand. He reached out to touch the fly ... and it buzzed!

NOT DEAD!

Jake screamed and ran to the door. He opened it. The fly shook a little, then it lazily flew out the door and off into the green trees, buzzing like a chainsaw.

Chris woke up, and asked sleepily, "What's wrong?"

That was freaky, Jake thought. *I am NOT going to think about flies today.*

Don't think about the swamp either!

"Nothing. Go back to sleep."

The cabin was heating up and it really did stink of socks. Jake was glad to leave, even if it was for some stupid swimming lessons with a bunch of kids he didn't know. He stuffed his sleeping bag and clothes into his backpack.

Chris rolled over. "See you later, Jake. Come by this afternoon if you want." Then he went back to sleep. Kate rolled over, snoring.

"Sure, okay, see you guys," Jake said.

He grabbed his backpack and padded quietly through the trees. He picked up his green bike from the Cuthberts' fence and rode along the laneway to his grandpa's.

It was really quiet. The sun was coming up, and the sky was pink and yellow behind the fields.

BUZZZZ! Jake squealed. A huge fly smashed right into the side of his head. It fell to the ground as soon as it hit him. It seemed dead for sure, this time. All six legs were across its chest.

Jake stopped his bike and rubbed the side of his head. The giant fly actually hurt.

I've never been hurt by a fly before. That's just not normal.

Jake reached down carefully. He wanted to put the fly into his shirt pocket to show to his grandpa. But suddenly he heard ...

... more buzzing!

And it was getting LOUDER.

He dropped the dead fly. He pumped the pedals of his bike as fast as he could. He didn't know what the buzzing was, and he did *not* want to find out!

The buzzing got louder. It sounded like a bunch of chainsaws coming his way.

Jake pedalled faster and faster down the lane, his legs a blur. He put his head down as he sprinted. He could have won medals, he was pedalling so fast. He was too scared to look behind him.

What could make a buzz as loud as that? I do NOT want to know!

"Hold up! Hold up there, boy!" Jake almost crashed into his grandpa. He steered his bike into the grass in front of his grandpa's house and fell to the ground, gasping for air.

Jake lay sprawled on the grass and looked up into an apple tree. It was filled with

monster flies. Millions of bug eyes looked down at him.

Then he passed out.

CHAPTER 8

JAKE FALLS IN

Jake woke up and blinked. It was quiet and the sun was shining on his face through the dusty living room window. Jake had never been in the farmhouse living room; it wasn't a place that anyone ever used. Usually he was in his bedroom or the kitchen, or in the basement TV room (cold rooms!) if he felt brave and there was absolutely nothing else to do.

He blinked again and looked at his grandpa's worried face. Gus's tongue-of-death lolled in the background.

"Jake. You scared me. I was just coming to get you, then you tore out of nowhere like you were being chased by hounds from hell!"

Jake had a cool cloth on his head. A drop of water rolled into his ear.

"What the heck happened to you?" His grandpa sounded worried. He sat at Jake's feet, leaning on the back of the couch.

What *did* happen to him? He wasn't even sure.

"I guess I didn't get enough sleep last night, Grandpa. I probably shouldn't go to swimming lessons this morning, sorry. I don't feel all that well."

"Okay. I'll call the pool and let them know you won't be there today. Then I think I'll call your mother."

"No! It's okay. You don't need to call Mom. I'm just tired. I'll take a nap this morning and I'll probably feel a lot better." Jake didn't want to bother his mother back in the city. Besides, huge flies the size of birds didn't happen all that often.

Something weird was happening. And possibly something quite *interesting*.

The last thing he wanted was to get his mom all worried and have to go back to the city just as things were getting exciting.

When his grandpa left the room to call the pool, Jake sat up and looked out the window at the apple tree.

No monster flies buzzed in the branches. No monster flies stared down at him.

He must have imagined it.

Jake rested on the couch a little longer, reading his grandpa's old fishing magazines. But pretty soon he got bored. He knew he had to do something or he'd curl up and die.

Like a giant fly? No!

He ran downstairs to watch TV in the basement. He tried to ignore the cold rooms. They weren't always creepy. When Jake's grandmother was alive, she used to store homemade jam and pickled vegetables in those rooms. Jake was just old enough to remember going downstairs with his grandma and seeing rows and rows and rows of glass jars full of delicious preserves. But most of the cold rooms had been empty since his grandmother died.

He tried not to think about the cold rooms.

He watched cartoons for a while, but the truth was he actually felt fine. He wasn't tired at all, but his grandpa wanted him to rest for the morning. Finally he couldn't stand it anymore. When twelve o'clock rolled around, he knew he had to do something or he was going to die of boredom.

So he made lunch.

Jake made tuna sandwiches and lemonade. He carefully opened the tuna tin and dumped it into a bowl. He broke it up with a fork. Then he put the tuna onto four bread slices on a paper plate, which he slapped into sandwiches. The lemonade was trickier. He had to open the frozen can and then dump it into a tall plastic pitcher. Then he had to add the water from the giant, upside down water-bottle dispenser beside the basement stairs. He could have used the horse-head pump outside, but it would have taken forever to fill the pitcher. The pumped water was fine, delicious even, but it did take a long time to pump it out of the ground. It was hard on your arms to pump a glass of water.

Finally, lunch was ready. He balanced the paper plate of sandwiches and the pitcher of lemonade with two cups on a tray and carefully went out the kitchen door and up to the field.

He found his grandpa wearing heavy gloves and goggles, digging a deep hole with a shovel. A square of pegs and string was laid out on the grass. It was the shape of the shed that Jake and his grandpa were going to build.

His grandpa stopped working when Jake came up with lunch. His grandpa seemed surprised and took off his goggles and gloves. He took a long, grateful drink of lemonade.

"Thanks Jake, that's really nice of you."

Then Jake and his grandpa sat and ate tuna sandwiches.

"What's that?" Jake asked between bites. He pointed at a machine in the grass. It looked like a giant corkscrew.

"Did I ever tell you about the time I opened a bottle of wine for a giant?" his grandpa said. He winked.

Jake felt a Grandpa story, no, a Grandpa *lie* coming on. So he said in his most no-nonsense voice, "No, Grandpa. Please, no stories. Yes, it looks like a giant corkscrew, but I know it's not. Please just tell me what it is. No stories. No exaggerations. No lies."

His grandpa looked a little hurt. "It *could* be a corkscrew for a giant's bottle of wine though, don't you think? Can't you imagine the size of the bottle, and how hard you'd have to turn it to get the cork out?"

"Sure, Grandpa, I guess I could imagine that. If I was a little kid. But I'm not. I'm twelve now, you know." Jake crossed his arms. He hoped it made him look older.

His grandpa looked so eager that Jake relented. He didn't want to hurt his grandpa's feelings. He sighed.

"Alright, Grandpa, sure. It *could* be a corkscrew for a giant bottle of wine. But how would you reach the top of the bottle with the corkscrew, and it would be heavy ... it would never work. You'd have to *be* a giant to use it. Do you have any giants around here?"

At that very moment a huge fly buzzed into Jake's face. His grandpa spluttered out lemonade and shooed the fly away. He suddenly looked serious.

"You're right, Jake. It would be impossible. It's not a corkscrew for a giant. It's called an auger. It digs big holes. I'm about to use it to make this hole deeper. Do you want to help?"

"Sure."

Jake's grandpa lifted the corkscrew-looking machine and put it into the partly dug hole. "Put on these gloves and these goggles. Okay, grab that handle and ... *push*." Jake and his grandpa each took a handle and turned the auger into the field. It was hard work, since the auger was heavy. It really did work like a giant corkscrew, churning into the ground and moving dirt out of the way.

Jake had to push against the handle with all his might then turn it far enough for his grandpa to grab and turn on his side. The auger slowly dug into the soil, a little deeper with each turn.

Oh yeah, I'm gonna have huge muscles after this, Jake thought. After ten minutes of struggling with the auger, the hole was deep enough for the post, and Jake's grandpa laid the heavy auger on the ground. Both of them were sweating. It was a pretty big hole.

"Okay, let's hook up Maggie. She can help us move the post into place," his grandpa said. He took off his gloves and goggles and headed toward the barn.

Jake walked over to an apple tree and flopped onto the grass. Gus woke up and licked him.

Jake scooted away from Gus's tongue-of-death across the grass … and his hand fell into nothingness.

Then his whole body followed.

Jake had fallen head first into the giant hole.

CHAPTER 9

DEATH BY POST HOLE

The post hole Jake and his grandpa just dug was deep. And DARK.

Jake was stuck in the hole, head down. All his weight rested on one hand stretched above his head.

"Help! HELP!" Jake shouted, but the hole swallowed his cries. He was yelling head down into the dark, sandy soil.

Who would hear him?

If he pointed his toes, his feet stuck out a little at the top. He kicked his legs wildly, trying to wriggle back out. But he was too far into the hole to get out that way.

Blood rushed to his head. His heart started to beat faster.

"Okay, stay calm. Breathe. It's okay. Help! Help!"

Jake was about to die head-down in a hole. Every time he struggled, dirt rained down on him, clogging his nose and mouth and eyes. Dirt was filling his ears. He could smell his own breath. He was slowly suffocating.

He felt faint. His eyes were so full of dirt he couldn't see properly. He swallowed and tried to blink dirt out of his eyes.

Then he saw it: something white and ghostly poking through the dirt at the bottom of the hole. He touched it. It was cool, and hard, and smooth.

What IS that? I'm going to die head down in a hole with some creepy white monster!

Suddenly he felt a tug on his leg. Then another. Something was tugging at his pant leg. He braced himself against the wall with his hand and pushed with all his might. He wriggled his back and legs, working himself upward.

Something kept tugging at his pant leg, pulling him. Slowly Jake inched up toward the light.

Who is helping me?

It was Gus!

Gus had grabbed onto Jake's pant leg and slowly tugged and tugged him. Jake could hear the dog grunting and whining. The old hound dog dug in all four paws, and with big jerks was slowly saving him.

Rocks and dirt and tree roots dug into Jake's flesh, his back and arms were scratched. His eyes were bursting, his head was pounding, and every muscle in his body screamed for fresh air.

Gus was a big, strong old dog, and he didn't let go until he saw Jake's face pop out of the hole. Jake rolled onto the grass, gasping, and looked up into the blue sky. Gus's lolling tongue reached down and licked his face. Jake didn't even mind. He threw his arms around the old dog's neck.

"You saved me, Gus," he breathed into the dog's smelly fur.

Gus barked as Jake's grandpa came up with Maggie in a harness. It was just like the old dog was trying to tell his master that something bad happened to his grandson.

Jake's grandpa patted Gus's head. "Settle down there, old boy. It's just me and Maggie … what the heck…?"

He looked at Jake, who was still gasping. He dropped Maggie's reins and got down on one creaky knee, resting his hand on Jake's shoulder. "Jake! What's wrong? Are you feeling sick again?"

Jake sat up. His face was all scratched and red, and he was gasping for air. He realized he must look really awful, with dirt and leaves all over his face and in his hair.

He stood up shakily and brushed himself off. "I'm okay, Grandpa. Gus saved me. I … I fell into the hole. Gus pulled me out."

They both looked over at the old dog, who was snapping at flies, normal sized ones, Jake noted. His grandpa took a deep breath and spoke very slowly.

"Jake, I don't know what you're thinking, sticking your head into a post hole! What was so interesting about a post hole? Really, you aren't right in the head sometimes. People have been known to die in post holes." He picked up Maggie's reins. Maggie was tugging at the grass with her big, chompy horse teeth.

That was the closest Jake ever came to hearing his grandpa get mad at him. He was a little shocked. Was it really that dangerous?

"Well, I was getting away from Gus, and I kind of just fell in. I'm sorry."

Jake looked down. He felt really bad. His poor grandpa. He should probably try not to die in the next two weeks. His grandpa would be in so much trouble with his mom if anything happened. He'd only been there one day and he'd already been scared to death and almost died in a stupid post hole.

"Sorry, Grandpa. You're right. I'll try to be more careful." Jake changed the subject. "I saw something down there at the bottom of the hole, though. It was white, a really white stone."

He waited, but his grandpa was silent. "Aren't you going to say something? Grandpa?"

But it was suddenly like his grandpa couldn't hear him. His whole face changed. He looked completely blank, like a white stone himself. He plunked down on the grass beside Gus and just sat there staring at Jake.

"Grandpa? Are you okay?"

After a long while his grandpa answered him, very quietly. "Jake, go fetch me a drink of water, please."

Jake nodded and rushed across the field into the kitchen. His heart fell: the water dispenser was empty. He'd used up all the water on the stupid lemonade. He hesitated for a moment. Go to the horse-head pump and take ten minutes to pump out a glass for his grandpa? Or load the water dispenser with a new bottle?

The new bottles were in the basement, in a cold room. They weighed almost as much as he did, and it would take forever for him to get one up the basement stairs and into the dispenser. He might not even be strong enough to load it into the dispenser, even if he *could* get it up the stairs. He'd never done it before.

Jake chose the horse-head pump. He grabbed a plastic cup and ran outside. He pumped, and pumped, and pumped, until finally a cool jet of pure water burst out onto his feet. Some of it got into the cup. He pumped and pumped, until he thought his arms were going to break.

Finally, he pumped a full cup of water. Jake carefully walked around the barn and back to his grandpa with the too-full plastic cup, trying not to spill a drop.

His grandpa gulped down the water then wiped his mouth. He looked better. He managed a squinty smile and got to his feet. He groaned a little as he straightened his knees and picked up Maggie's forgotten reins. Maggie snorted and pulled her head up. Her leather harness squeaked as she stomped her front legs.

"Okay, Jake. Just try to be more careful. No more post holes. Let's take Maggie into town. Ice cream?"

Jake nodded and followed his grandfather and the horse. As he walked past the fateful post hole, he gasped.

It was full of dirt. His grandpa had refilled the hole. He must have done it when Jake went to get him the water. Jake looked at his grandpa's back as he climbed into the cart behind the old horse.

Why did his grandpa *fill in the post hole?* What on earth was DOWN THERE?

CHAPTER 10

MRS. CODY ISN'T TALKING

Jake and his grandpa took the horse and the cart into town. Maggie clopped slowly along the leafy streets. She held up traffic, but no one seemed to mind. A "Slow Moving Vehicle" sign was on the back of the cart, so people knew to be careful.

The town Jake's grandpa lived near was a sleepy little place most of the time, but in late summer the main street was filled with tourists. People strolled down the pretty boulevard eating homemade ice cream and buying farm antiques. Every afternoon in August, musicians played on the bandstand at the middle of the park.

Today, three men in kilts were playing bagpipes.

The sound made Jake think of drowning cats, but the tourists seemed to like it. Teenagers were sitting on tree boughs; little kids were on their dads' shoulders. Everyone wanted to hear the bagpipes. Jake wasn't sure why. He could remember the men with bagpipes, the tourists strolling along on a pleasant summer afternoon eating ice cream, ever since he was little.

Jake's grandpa slowed Maggie to a stop in front of the town pharmacy. He gave Jake some money and told him to go get them both ice cream. Jake hopped out of the cart and crossed the street.

The ice cream store was next to the library, and both places were really busy on such a hot day. Jake decided that was probably because both places had air conditioning. Jake waited in line and got two ice cream cones, both vanilla. He and his grandpa were exactly the same in some ways. As he walked back past the library with the ice cream, his heart skipped a beat.

A big sign on the library steps said, 100 YEARS OF OUR HISTORY! COME IN TO FIND OUT THE TRUTH BEHIND SOME OF OUR TALLEST TALES.

Jake looked across the street. His grandpa was sitting in the cart, talking to another old man. Gus sat beside him, too hot to move, and Maggie hung her head in the sun, looking sleepy. They didn't see Jake.

Jake ran up the library steps and poked his head inside. It was quiet, cool, and dark in the library, and it smelled of books. He looked around and spotted a display case near the librarian's desk. It had a sign that read 100 YEARS OF TOWN HISTORY! There were some photos and books on stands, too. He walked over for a closer look.

There were newspaper clippings and ancient pictures of farmers with old-fashioned farm equipment.

One photo was of a huge pumpkin beside a smiling farmer. The caption read, "Charles Bywater grows 200 lb. pumpkin!" Another photo was of an enormous black horse beside a woman who looked tiny standing next to it. The caption read, "Mrs. Albert Hodges breeds national champion, 18-hand stallion." Another photo was of an old, stooped man in a long jacket, holding garden shears. "Local Girl Goes Missing in Gardener's Maze," the headline read.

Wow, this town IS strange.

Then Jake stopped at a story with a photo of a beautiful golden retriever dog beside an old, rich-looking man. The headline read, "Local Man Killed Looking for Dog."

What a beautiful dog, Jake thought.

Jake kept scanning, then his eyes stopped at a newspaper clipping that made his heart thump harder.

The headline read, "Mrs. Edwina Fingles Missing, Presumed Dead." It was dated December 12, 1908. There was a photo of a sad-looking little old lady in a bonnet. Jake read the first paragraph of the story:

> *Edwina Fingles, 76, has been missing for four days. Her son, Thomas Fingles, contacted local constables after he visited his mother and found the house empty and the back door swinging open. According to her son, Edwina loved the fields and the swampland at the back of the farm. Residents should contact the local constabulary if they see any sign of Mrs. Fingles.*

Jake gulped.

Swampland? Little old lady gone missing?

Something touched his shoulder.

Jake screamed.

"Young man, shhh!" said a stern-looking lady. She had a name badge on. It read, MRS. CODY, LIBRARIAN.

"You must be Jake McGregor," she said. "I know your grandparents well. I was best friends with your grandma when we were schoolgirls. I spent a lot of time on your grandpa's farm when I was a young woman. I knew your mom, too, when she was little. How is she?"

"Ummm. Hi, Mrs. Cody. My mom's well, thanks, we live in the city now. Sorry I screamed, but you scared me," Jake said.

"Yes, scary stuff, isn't it?" Mrs. Cody said, pointing at the newspaper clipping of Edwina Fingles. "Poor Edwina, she was never found. They say she just wandered off and got lost in the ..."

Don't say swamp!

"... swamp."

Jake gulped again and nodded. "Yeah, I heard that story." Then he thought of something. "But what about the story of the giant hand? That story about the giant corpse hand turning up in a field around here a long time ago?"

Mrs. Cody shifted her weight, crossed her arms, and leaned against the board with the newspaper clippings. She was a big lady, so she blocked the board completely. She looked down at Jake and grew stern again. "That's just a spooky old ghost story, Jake. No one ever said *that* was true."

She really did look scary. But Jake wasn't satisfied.

"But *you* did, you said it was true, on a ghost walk last year. My friend told me."

"Well, there are stories, and then there are *stories*, Jake. Do you see a newspaper clipping on the wall about a giant hand?"

Jake looked at the wall, but Mrs. Cody was leaning against pretty much all of the clippings, blocking them from his view, so he couldn't check.

She went on: "Don't you think a giant hand in someone's field might make it into the newspapers? And where would a giant hand come from? Did it fall out of the sky? And where did it go? No, that's just ghost walk scary talk, nothing real about that story. Just put that out of your head."

Jake was about to protest when Mrs. Cody pointed at his ice cream. She said, "No food allowed in the library, Jake, sorry. You're melting onto the floor. Be sure and say hello to your grandpa for me."

Mrs. Cody was right. The ice cream was running down Jake's hand. He had no choice but to leave. He thanked the librarian and headed back out into the heat.

He peeked back at her just before he left the cool library for good, and gasped. When she thought no one was looking, Mrs. Cody pulled a newspaper clipping from the board and tucked it into her pocket.

Jake couldn't believe his eyes! What was she hiding?

CHAPTER 11

NO FLIES ON US

The next morning, Jake went to his swimming lesson. It actually wasn't that bad. The other kids were pretty nice, and the teachers were teenagers so they weren't too strict. Jake was surprised when the hour-long lesson was over.

The rest of the day he played with Gus in the front yard, visited Maggie in the barn, and rode his bike up and down the lane or into the field. His grandpa didn't mention building the shed again.

The big auger shone in the sun.

In the middle of the hot afternoon, a minibike roared up the lane. Jake looked up from reading in the hammock on the big front porch and waved. Kate was driving, and Chris waved back from behind her. Kate parked the tiny machine.

"Hey, guys." Jake lifted himself a little from the hammock.

"Hey, Jake," Chris said. He wrestled his blond head out of his skull helmet. "You want to come fishing? We're going back to the creek."

Swamp!

"Um, okay. Now?"

"Yeah, go ask your grandpa."

Jake shifted from the hammock and slowly swung his feet onto the porch.

Kate pointed over at the stakes laid out in the shape of the abandoned shed. "Hey, what's that auger doing over there?"

"My grandpa was building a shed."

"Was?"

"Yeah. He kind of lost interest. I'll be right back." He went to look for his grandpa and found him napping in his bedroom. Gus lay on the floor. He thumped his tail at Jake but didn't move.

Jake made a "shhhh" at Gus, then left his grandpa a note on the kitchen table.

"Grandpa, I went fishing with Chris and Kate. Back for dinner. Jake."

He went and got his bike from the barn, then the three friends headed back toward the creek. They found a perfect spot under the trees beside the little stream. The twins set their rods, then Chris brought out a bag of trail mix he made: peanuts, granola, raisins, and sunflower seeds.

"That was a crazy story about the giant hand," Jake said, his mouth full of trail mix.

Chris rolled his eyes, but Kate nodded. "I know. Mrs. Cody scared us when she told it last year at the ghost walk."

"What's a ghost walk, anyway?"

"Well, you walk around and tell ghost stories at haunted or creepy parts of town," Kate said. "And believe me, our town is super-haunted and weird. At least judging by the number of creepy stories Mrs. Cody told us."

"Where were you when she told the story about the ghost hand?" Jake asked.

"Oh, I think beside the library. Some of the stories were about places too far away to visit, or too mysterious, or they didn't really know exactly where something happened. They're just strange stories she wanted to share."

Jake shivered. "There's a whole bunch of newspaper clippings in the library about creepy stuff."

"Like what?" Kate asked.

"Some of them were about huge horses and giant pumpkins and things. Then one was about an old lady, Edwina Fingles. She got lost in the swamp, way back in 1908 or something." Jake looked sideways at Kate.

She nodded. "Yeah, that one seems kind of true, doesn't it? Sometimes it's hard to tell what's real and what isn't around here. This town is a little weird."

This time it was Jake's turn to nod. *No kidding!*

"There weren't any newspaper stories about a giant hand, though," he said quietly. "And when I asked Mrs. Cody about it, she acted really ... sneaky."

Kate laughed. "She's really nice, Jake! What do you mean 'sneaky'?"

"I'm not sure. She used her body to block all the clippings I hadn't seen yet. When I left, I'm sure she snuck one of the clippings off the wall."

"Weird," Kate whispered softly.

Jake said, "I want to go back to the library.

Do you guys think you could get your dad to take us tomorrow?"

The twins nodded. "Oh yeah, he always wants us to go to the library." Kate rolled her eyes.

Chris piped up, "I have books to take back. Let's go tomorrow for sure. It's supposed to rain, anyway."

"Good," Jake said, then he thought of something else. "Hey, have you guys ever seen white rocks around here? Like really white, white stones deep down in the ground?"

Chris shrugged. "White rocks? Nope. Kate?"

Kate thought for a minute. "No. Dad dug a huge hole last year for the new kitchen sunroom, but there weren't any white stones down there. Why?"

Jake didn't answer right away. "Well, I saw this really white stone in the bottom of a post hole my grandpa and I dug."

"Where?" Kate asked.

"Near the auger you saw. It was a hole for the shed, for a post. I actually fell in the hole. Gus dragged me out."

Kate shrugged. "No white stones around here, Jake. If you want, we can help you look for more."

"Yeah. Okay. Oh, and what about *flies*?"

Kate shrugged again. "What about them? It's farmland. There are always lots of flies around a farm. They like cow poop." She looked at Jake like he was crazy.

"No, I mean big flies, like *really* big flies. Flies the size of birds that make a sound like a chainsaw?"

Kate laughed, and it was Chris's turn to look at Jake like he wasn't making sense.

"No, that's crazy talk Jake. There are definitely no flies around here the size of birds. I think we would have noticed them." The twins looked at each other briefly, like they were a little worried about their friend from the city.

Kate cleared her throat. "The fish aren't biting," she said. "Let's go back. I'm starving."

The twins and Jake rode back toward the farmhouse.

When they were gone, a giant fly buzzed over the riverbank. It dropped into the grass where they had been sitting and found a sunflower seed. For a moment, a horrible gobbling and sucking sound filled the air.

Then the fly buzzed lazily back into the woods.

CHAPTER 12

WHAT DOES GRANDPA KNOW?

Jake sat looking over the field. The sun was going down, and it was quiet and peaceful. Jake's grandpa was smoking a pipe in a lawn chair nearby, reading the paper.

Jake stroked Gus's head. "Grandpa?" he finally said.

His grandfather put down his paper and looked up. "Yup?"

"Grandpa..." Jake wasn't sure how to continue.

"Somethin' on your mind there, Jake?"

"Well, it's just that the other night at Kate and Chris's, Kate told this crazy story...."

"… about a giant hand?" his grandpa finished. When Jake looked surprised, his grandpa said, "Chris told me when I came to remind you about swimming, remember?"

"Oh yeah, he did mention it, didn't he? Well, it's just that Kate seemed so sure it was true and Chris seemed so sure it wasn't. And then at the library yesterday, I met Mrs. Cody … she says hello, by the way … and I asked her about the giant hand, and she really seemed like she was hiding something. She put one of the newspaper clippings in her pocket when she thought I wasn't looking. I was just wondering if you ever heard that story … about the giant hand?"

His grandpa sighed. "You know, Jake, you probably shouldn't believe everything you hear. And Mabel Cody is a lovely lady, great friends with your grandma and me for years, but she gets the kids all riled up with those ghost walks every summer. Just ask yourself this, Jake: how would a giant hand turn up in someone's back field? Where'd it come from?"

"Yeah, sure, I guess. But you *have* heard the story, though?" Jake went on. He was determined to get his grandpa to tell him what he knew. His grandpa sighed and leaned his old head against the back of the chair.

"Yes, Jake, I've heard that story. It's an old scary story from around these parts. But honestly, a giant hand? Who thought *that* up? Look, like I said, this town is *weird*. People are bored, they don't have much to do, so they think up crazy stories to spook each other with. Poor old Edwina Fingles goes missing, and suddenly we have a swamp creature. But a giant hand? I'm with Christopher Cuthbert on this one. Just nonsense."

His grandpa stretched and sighed. Conversation over.

"Go get the backgammon board and we'll have a game out here before the sun goes down." Jake went inside to get the game board. But he could have sworn that his grandpa changed the subject a little too quickly. He didn't even try to start one of his crazy "did-I-ever-tell-you-about-the-time" stories.

Which wasn't like him. It wasn't like him at all.

CHAPTER 13

ACCESS DENIED

The next day was rainy. At ten o'clock Mr. Cuthbert's big black van pulled up and Jake climbed in. He waved goodbye to his grandpa and Gus waiting beside the road.

Chris and Kate were sitting in the back seats, so Jake got the front seat beside their dad. He couldn't help but notice that Chris sat beside a huge stack of books. Kate didn't seem to have any.

"Are those the books you're taking back?" Jake pointed. It was a huge pile.

"Yeah. They're mostly about ancient Egypt, but there are a few Hardy Boys stories in here, too." He picked a book out of the pile and handed it to Jake. The blue cover read, *The Hardy Boys: The Twisted Claw*.

The image of a twisted, bony hand made Jake shudder.

A giant twisted hand in a farmer's field!

Jake handed the book back to Chris. "Thanks, I'm really not into mysteries."

Mr. Cuthbert drove slowly along the country lanes. Even though it was raining, Jake liked looking out the window at the late summer fields. The apples in the trees were ripe, the wheat in the fields was high, and almost everything was ready to go to market. Jake liked the clean smell of the air, too. Sometimes he thought it might not be *so* bad to live in the country, like Kate and Chris. Maybe he could get a mini-bike....

Then Mr. Cuthbert pulled the van up in front of the library. The steps were slippery with rain, and the three friends had to run carefully up to the big wooden door.

Mr. Cuthbert yelled, "I'll be back in an hour," then he drove off.

Jake opened the big, wide door with a creak, and the friends stepped into the quiet, dark library. Water streamed down the glass windows outside, but inside the library it was dark, and silent. Since it was Saturday morning and raining, nobody was there yet.

Jake walked to the front desk. Another librarian was working today, not Mrs. Cody, which was probably a good thing considering what Jake was looking for.

"Excuse me, I'm wondering where the 100 Years of Our History display went?" Jake pointed to the corner where the sign had been and where all the newspaper clippings were stuck to the board. "It was here a few days ago," he added.

The librarian looked up at Jake, and he got the distinct impression that she really didn't want to be disturbed. She was much younger than Mrs. Cody, but she didn't look nearly as friendly.

"Oh, that was on loan from the city archives. We had to return it yesterday."

"Oh." Jake stood there, not sure what to do next. Chris Cuthbert struggled up to the desk with two armloads of books.

"Hi, Mrs. Strathroy," Chris said in his most polite voice.

Mrs. Strathroy smiled. "Hi, Chris! Good to see you. Returning all these today? Or are there any renewals?"

"Nope, Mrs. Strathroy. I'm returning them all, thanks." Then Chris and Mrs. Strathroy got into a five-minute conversation about which book Chris liked best. It was a Hardy Boys book, the one he had showed Jake: *The Twisted Claw*.

Then Chris smiled at the librarian again. "We're actually a bit disappointed that the 100 Years of Our History display is gone, Mrs. Strathroy. We were hoping to do a little research and start our local history projects for school this year."

Jake and Kate nodded solemnly behind Chris.

Great thinking! Local history projects! Brilliant!

"Oh! What a great idea." Mrs. Strathroy beamed. "I can't show you the original newspaper clippings since that's all been boxed and moved to the archive museum in the city." The three friends tried not to look too disappointed. Jake felt his heart sink.

"But I *can* show you how to use the archive on the librarian's computer. All the stories we used for the historical display are in there. It will show you scanned images of the original newspapers. Some of them are over one hundred years old, so you can imagine the quality isn't perfect. Shall I sign you in and show you how to use it? It's right over there." She pointed at a sleek new machine behind a huge librarian's desk in the far corner.

"Mrs. Strathroy, that's so nice of you! Thank you, we really appreciate it." Chris smiled again at Mrs. Strathroy, and before they knew it the three friends were seated at the librarian's computer, looking up historical articles from the display. Chris sat at the screen while Jake and Kate looked over his shoulder.

Mrs. Strathroy found them the right folder, then left them to their "history projects." Chris opened the folder with a click. The titles of hundreds of newspaper articles popped up. Kate leaned over her brother's shoulder and whispered, "You are such a geek. Thank you for being such a geek, from the bottom of my heart."

"Yeah, Chris, thanks. Where would we be without you?" Jake suddenly realized that it might just pay to be charming and well-read.

They started looking through the file names of each newspaper clipping. The entries were strange and, frankly, a little disturbing.

"Giant hail stone kills McGready horse: 1912"

"Frequent fog patches cause panic among local pigs: 1907"

"Record-breaking pumpkin owner dies eating pumpkin pie: 1897"

"Famous blueberry jam poisons dozens at fall fair: 1921"

"Local honey producer drowns in honey vat: 1917"

"Man, this town IS weird!" Kate said after Chris had scrolled down a few pages.

Then Chris said, "Hey, look!" and pointed at a folder that said, *"Lady goes missing in swamp: 1908."*

"That must be the Edwina Fingles story. Maybe we're getting close," Jake said, excited. Chris kept scrolling.

"Circles found in dust bowl crops: 1932"

"Farmer claims four-ton boulder in his field mysteriously moved 300 feet overnight: 1930"

"Family hears spectral train on long-abandoned track: 1918"

"Fournette ghost walks highway looking for lost dog: 1912"

"Mysterious maze and local girl vanish into thin air: 1913"

Then Chris jabbed his finger at the screen. "Here!"

The file read, *"Giant hand-like structure found in farmer's field: 1913"*

"That's it! Click on it, Chris!" Jake could barely contain his excitement. Chris clicked on the file ... and a message popped up: USER BLOCKED. The three friends groaned. Chris tried again, but the same message popped up. "User Blocked. Access Denied."

"Wait," Chris said. "You can sort of see the newspaper clipping underneath the blocked message. It's a little hard to see. But there ... it's one of the farmer's feet, and looks like a view of the back door of the kitchen maybe." Chris squinted and moved in closer to the screen. "Under the picture it says, '... father and son discovered this morni ...' That's all you can see. Here. Look, Jake."

Jake switched places with Chris and leaned in close to the computer screen. He peered hard. The big "USER BLOCKED, ACCESS DENIED" banner covered most of the image and pretty much all of the article, but Chris was right. He *could* see a tiny bit of the picture and read a little of the caption. Jake looked. He could see feet, a bit of grass, a tiny bit of back door … then his heart started to race. He saw something.…

He was about to tell Kate and Chris what he saw in the picture when a loud voice spoke behind them.

"What are YOU doing on the librarian's computer? This isn't for you!" It was Mrs. Cody. "Mrs. Strathroy had no right to let you peek through our files. Shoo." She reached over and snapped off the computer screen. She sent the three friends scurrying away, then she went to scold Mrs. Strathroy.

Kate, Chris, and Jake gathered at the library door and waited for Mr. Cuthbert to pick them up. When they were away from the prying eyes and ears of Mrs. Cody, Jake whispered to his friends.

"I saw something in the picture."

"What? What did you see?" Kate breathed. Chris leaned in to listen.

"I saw a *pump*. A horse-head pump. There's only one, and it's on Grandpa's farm. The picture *had* to be taken there!"

The twins looked at Jake, and Kate let out a long, low whistle.

"Looks like your grandpa might know more than you think," Chris finally whispered.

Jake nodded. "Yeah, he knows something alright."

But what?

CHAPTER 14

GIANT FLY TORNADO

After swimming lessons the next day, Jake's grandpa went shopping and left Jake alone with Gus for a few hours.

Jake and Gus wandered around the barn. Gus chased barn cats and Jake stroked Maggie's nose. He climbed in the hay and swung around the old rafters. It was fun for an hour. It gave him time to think about what to do next. It also kept his mind off what he'd seen, what he was *sure* he saw, in the library archives.

A horse-head pump in the picture about the giant hand!

He just wasn't sure how to ask his grandpa about it.

After a while, Jake noticed his bike parked beside the barn. He called Gus, then he rode his bike into the field. It was a warm, sunny, beautiful day. Gus ran beside him and barked into the wind. Halfway to the woods, Jake stopped pedalling and sat quietly, listening to the field sounds.

There was a blackbird singing in the long grass and the sound of wind in the trees.

There was the distant croak of a frog in the woods.

There was a ... BUZZZZZZZZ.

Jake shrieked and ducked just as a giant fly buzzed over the top of his head. Two more flies came right at him. Gus started barking. Jake jumped on his bike and pedalled as fast as he could back to the house. He didn't even park the bike back in the barn, he just left it beside the back door. Then boy and dog ran into the farmhouse and Jake slammed the door.

Jake sat in the kitchen, too scared to look outside or do anything, until he heard the sound of the pickup truck. When his grandpa walked into the kitchen with the groceries, Jake breathed a sigh of relief. Gus barked.

"Are we glad to see you!" Jake called. His grandpa put two paper bags full of groceries on the kitchen table. They started unpacking everything.

"Anything exciting happen here while I was gone?" his grandpa asked. Jake was thinking about how to answer when his grandpa looked out the kitchen window and frowned.

"What the heck? Jake, please put the rest of these groceries away."

His grandpa walked out the back door. Jake stood with a jar of pickles in his hand and watched his grandpa stride across the back field.

There was a black cloud swirling over the grass. It was like a tiny tornado, taller than a man, swirling and moving quickly toward the farmhouse. It was too far away for Jake to see very clearly, but it was moving fast. Jake saw his grandpa reach the swirling cloud ... and DISAPPEAR!

Then Jake heard him shriek.

Jake dropped the jar of pickles and ran into the field. He ran fast across the bumpy grass, right into a dark, buzzing cloud of ... giant flies!

Monster flies smacked into Jake's head. They buzzed into his eyes and nose and ears. They were so loud, he couldn't think.

This is so GROSS!

Huge, buzzing flies covered his whole body. Sticky bug feet stuck to his skin. Hairy bug faces flew into his face. Huge bug wings brushed against his lips and eyes.

He wanted to scream, but he was too scared to open his mouth. He could hear Gus barking and barking nearby. The old dog was too wise to jump into the bug whirlwind, though, Jake noticed.

If I EAT one of these things, I will die of disgust! Jake pushed further into the bug tornado, trying to find his grandpa. He was in there somewhere; Jake could hear him yelling. Jake dug deep into the bravest place he could find inside himself and groped through the swirling mass of creepy, monstrous bugs. He went further into the bug cloud, reaching and grabbing until he caught his grandpa's arm.

His grandpa started yelling at the top of his lungs. He didn't seem to care if the flies flew into his mouth.

"Leave me alone! Just go away!" he screamed. Jake wasn't sure if his grandpa was yelling at him or the flies.

Jake tugged on his grandpa's hand. It was dark and loud in the bug swarm, and …

everything was crawling. Jake clamped his mouth shut tighter and tucked his chin to his neck. He squinted his eyes almost shut. The wings and feet and bodies of the giant flies were almost blinding; it was like struggling through a snowstorm ... a bugstorm. Buzzing wings brushed his skin, huge bug eyes flew at him, bugs crawled all over every inch of him.

Walking into the bug tornado was the single grossest thing he'd ever done.

Jake tugged and tugged, but his grandpa seemed stuck in the buzzing cloud. It was almost like the flies were keeping him there. His grandpa yelled and waved his free hand at the bugs. Jake pulled and pulled, until slowly his grandpa started to move toward the house and out of the swirling mass. Step by step, Jake dragged and pulled his grandpa until they crossed the field and stepped back into the house. Gus barked and barked and jumped everywhere, snapping at flies.

Finally, they stood in the kitchen, gasping. Jake made his grandpa sit down, then handed him a cup of water from the full dispenser.

"Grandpa? Grandpa, what *was* that? Where did those giant flies come from?"

"I don't want to talk about it! No more ghost story questions! No more crazy made-up gibberish about a giant hand. I'm going to bed, Jake. I need a nap." Jake couldn't believe his ears. He looked at his grandfather in horror. He felt his voice rise.

"WHAT? How can you not want to talk about what just happened?" Jake had never yelled at his grandpa before, but he couldn't help it.

But it was like his grandpa didn't hear him. Instead, he took Gus, went into his bedroom, and shut the door. Jake knocked on his door, then banged on it.

"Grandpa! What's going on! What *was* that ... bug cloud?" he yelled, but his grandpa ignored him. Jake didn't know what to do. He stood helplessly outside his grandpa's shut door. He placed his forehead against the wall.

Why doesn't Grandpa want to talk about the bugs? Why was he yelling at the flies to leave him alone? If he WAS yelling at the flies, not at me?

Jake slumped to the floor outside his grandpa's room and thought about flies.

A few minutes later a voice said through the door, "Your turn to make whatever you want for dinner, Jake. Run and play, I'm tired. No more. No more questions." Jake didn't want to upset his grandpa any more, and the old man sounded tired. So tired. He made a decision.

"Okay, Grandpa. I'll … I'll go and watch TV."

He slowly left his grandfather's door.

Things were getting very, very weird around there.

He cautiously looked out the back window, but the fly cloud had disappeared. The field was green, the sky was blue, and it was like nothing had happened.

Jake listened closely, but his grandpa and Gus were asleep. He checked the time. It was ten minutes after three. His grandpa sometimes slept until dinnertime, and tonight was Jake's turn to cook, so he might not get up until after five o'clock. Jake made a quick decision. He wrote a note to his grandpa and left it on the kitchen table. He screwed up all his courage and peeked into the back field, again.

No flies. He ran out the back door and grabbed his bike.

Jake wanted answers. And if he wanted answers, he'd have to dig. And to dig, he needed help.

He needed Chris and Kate.

CHAPTER 15

BACK DOWN THE HOLE

Fifteen minutes later, Jake was standing in the back field. Chris and Kate were standing beside him, both with their hands on their hips. Jake's bike and the twins' mini-bike were behind them.

The three of them looked at the auger.

"Looks sharp," Kate said.

"Heavy, too," Chris added, scratching his head.

"Yeah, but the three of us should be able to use it," Jake said. "My grandpa and I used it a few days ago. I know how."

He showed Chris and Kate how to hold the handles, and they dragged the heavy old-fashioned machine over to the refilled post hole.

"This looks like fresh dirt," Kate said.

"Yeah, it is. This is the post hole I fell into. This is where I saw the white stone at the bottom."

"Okay, let's do it!" Kate said, and they hoisted the heavy auger into place. Chris took one handle, Jake and Kate took the other.

"One, two, THREE!" Chris yelled. They pushed and pulled on three. The auger bit into the fresh dirt.

"One, two, THREE!" Chris yelled again. It took twenty minutes of hard, back-breaking turning. It definitely took longer with three kids than it had with Jake and his grandpa. But the auger slowly dug a fresh hole, until Jake thought his arms would break. All three friends were in a sweat when the auger finally hit the bottom of the hole.

The machine made a grinding sound. They pulled the auger out of the hole and laid it on the grass. All three were panting, harder than Gus ever did.

Jake peered down the hole.

Dark.

Chris brought a flashlight and rope from

the mini-bike storage box under the seat. He shone the light into the bottom of the hole, and there it was. A glint of white!

"See! It's white down there!" Jake shouted.

"Yeah, I see it too," Kate said.

"Yeah. Weird. You were right, Jake," Chris added, scratching his head.

"Okay, so you two tie the rope to my feet. I'm going down there," Jake said. He peeled off his sweatshirt and tied the rope around his ankles.

He lowered himself on his stomach and wriggled toward the hole, head first. Chris and Kate slowly lowered the rope. Jake shone the flashlight ahead of him.

"Okay, lower me down. More! A little more! More. Okay, stop! I'm at the bottom." His voice sounded really far away to Kate and Chris.

Jake was deep into the hole. It was scary down there, with dirt closing in on him on all sides. He tried hard not to think of graves and coffins. It was a little damp too, and smelled like leaves and ...

... swamp!

He could smell wet earth and rotting worms. His face was a few inches from the bottom. Dirt fell into his mouth, his ears, his eyes. His heart beat harder. It was creepy, quiet, and dark down at the bottom of the hole. He started to feel a little faint. He'd have to work fast.

He felt a million miles away from the surface. His grandpa was right — someone could really die down there.

He didn't have time to be scared. He had to concentrate. He used his left hand to hold the flashlight, and with his right hand he dug at the dirt. He scratched and clawed, and dug until ...

... there it was, a beautiful white stone. It was dazzling in the gloom at the bottom of the hole. He dug at it with his right hand, trying to get his fingers around it. But it was too big — there were no sides.

So he scratched at it, and knocked on it, and tried his best to move it, but the white rock wouldn't budge. The blood rushed to his head, and he was feeling faint.

"Hey, pull me out! Pull me up now!"

Kate and Chris backed up and started pulling him out of the hole, just like Gus had a few days before. Jake's shirt rode up his back, and dirt and rocks scratched his skin as he travelled upward. When he reached the top, he rolled onto the grass, breathing fresh air in big gulps.

"I've never been so happy to see the sky," Jake whispered.

Kate knelt down beside him. "Did you get the stone? What is it?"

"No, I couldn't dig it out. It's too big. It's really stuck down there."

Kate and Chris both took a turn. They were lowered into the hole to see if they could dig out the white stone, but no one could budge the rock. Everyone got scratches on their arms and legs and backs.

They were all exhausted after that. It was almost five o'clock when they finally gave up. Jake didn't want his grandfather to wake up and find him out in the field playing in post holes again. With Chris and Kate's help, he refilled the hole with dirt. It was a lot faster and easier to refill a post hole with a shovel and dirt than it was to dig one with the auger.

The twins and Jake walked back to the farmhouse together.

"Should we try again?" Chris asked.

"No."

"Why not?"

"Because I'm beginning to think that nothing can budge that rock."

"Maybe it's chalk or something? My dad says the fields around here are really chalky." This was Chris talking, but even he didn't sound convinced.

"It's not chalk," Jake said.

"Then what is it?" Kate asked.

"I don't know, but it reminds me of something," Jake said vaguely.

The twins put on their helmets.

"Thanks anyway, guys."

"Okay, see you, Jake. Let's go fishing tomorrow."

It was the strangest thing, but as his friends drove away, Jake felt like something BIG was about to happen. Something strange and upsetting that he had somehow set in motion and he was now helpless to stop.

He was right.

CHAPTER 16

CHALK AND CHEESE SANDWICHES

Chris and Kate left with a roar of the mini-bike. This time it was loud enough to wake up his grandpa, who came down to the kitchen with Gus, looking hungry.

"When's dinner there, Jake?" his grandpa said with a stretch.

"I'll start the grilled cheese sandwiches," Jake answered. He really wanted to ask his grandpa about the flies, but he'd have to time it. He didn't want his grandpa to get all quiet again. Or upset.

"Did I ever tell you about the time I made grilled cheese sandwiches for the Queen of

England?" his grandpa asked. He was sitting at the kitchen table, looking well-rested and happy, while Jake stood cooking at the stove. Jake didn't turn around.

"No, Grandpa. You didn't."

But you could *tell me about the giant fly tornado!*

His grandpa started a long story about how he was once a short-order cook on a riverboat in Ottawa. He was cooking for a summer, the same summer that the Queen of England came to visit. She wanted a grilled cheese sandwich; she'd never had one, and she'd heard that it was a Canadian delicacy. On and on the story went.

Jake was barely listening. How was he going to talk to his grandpa about the giant hand? About the flies? His grandpa said he didn't want to talk about it. Jake was concentrating hard, trying to come up with a plan, and stopped paying attention to what he was doing. He was making the first grilled cheese sandwiches of his life. He thought if he had to eat spaghetti or hot dogs one more day, he'd die.

But he stared out the window at the horse-head pump a little too long....

"JAKE! Watch what you're doing!" his grandpa yelled. Jake came back to his senses and clicked off the smoking stove. He burned one side of the sandwiches and undercooked the other, and the cheese didn't melt inside. But his grandpa didn't even seem to notice. They both sat at the table and ate in silence since his grandpa had finished his unlikely story about the queen's grilled cheese sandwiches.

Jake drank a glass of milk with his dinner. His grandpa had a root beer. Gus lay at their feet, biting his paws.

It all seemed pretty normal. But Jake was wiggly. He wanted to talk. He *needed* to talk about the swirling cloud of giant flies. About the white stone.

And the picture in the archives with the horse-head pump.

Finally he blurted out, "Grandpa, where'd those flies come from? And what's the white stone at the bottom of the post hole?"

His grandpa put one cheek on a fist and leaned against the table. "Have you heard about the time I discovered the sacred white wishing stones?" his grandpa said. He had a glint in his eye.

"No, Grandpa, no more stories! I'm serious. What's that white stone? It reminds me of something."

"Or did you ever hear my story about the great Fly Spirit that visits people with hordes of flies that clean up unwanted manure?" His grandpa was still grinning, but Jake was getting mad.

"Grandpa, it's really time to stop telling me stupid stories! I want the truth! Is it so hard to tell me the truth about what's going on around here?"

"I have no idea what you're talking about, Jake," his grandpa said, sitting up straight. He had an innocent look on his face. But Jake also thought he looked maybe a little ... worried. Or possibly sneaky.

"Yes, you do know what I'm talking about. You filled in the hole. You must have known there was something down there, something you didn't want me to see. Something white and creepy."

"I didn't want you to fall into any more holes, Jake. And I didn't see anything down there, just dirt, although the soil is chalky around here...." His grandfather trailed off. But he turned away and wouldn't look at his grandson.

He really looked like someone who was hiding something.

"But what about the flies, Grandpa? You can't deny those exist. You almost got carried away in a whirling cloud of them out in the field, and they're everywhere. Big, awful flies that buzz like a chainsaw."

"I only saw a cloud of bugs, Jake, not enormous flies," his grandfather answered quietly. But he kept his eyes down.

Jake nodded slowly, then said, "You tell stories all the time, Grandpa, but this is one story you *don't* want to tell me. Why?"

"I have no idea what you mean," his grandpa said again. Boy, could he be stubborn.

"I think you know, Grandpa. I think you know exactly what I mean."

They looked at each other for a moment. Jake couldn't read the expression on the old man's face. He didn't like upsetting his grandpa, but he had to find out the *truth*. He was beginning to figure it out … he had a terrible idea he already KNEW the truth.…

After a long silence Jake spoke again. Everything was suddenly perfectly clear, and he spoke like a grown-up who knew the beginning, middle, and end of the story. "There are gross, enormous flies disturbed from a long rest swarming all over the place. And it's not a white stone down there. I know exactly what it is, though. I've seen it before."

Jake held his grandpa in a long stare then finally said, "It's *bone* at the bottom of the hole, isn't it, Grandpa?"

CHAPTER 17

FOURTH COLD ROOM ON THE LEFT

Jake's grandpa opened his eyes wide and guffawed. "Bone? BONE? Where'd you get a crazy idea like that, Jake? Do you think that I've got bodies buried all over the field?"

"No," Jake said quietly. "Not *bodies*. *Bod-y*. Just one. Or part of one. The skeleton of a giant hand."

Jake's grandpa fell silent and suddenly wouldn't look up.

Jake went on. "It was *this* field, wasn't it? *Your* dad and grandpa woke up to loud buzzing. *They* had to cover their faces because of the giant flies. *They* buried the rotting corpse hand to hide it forever."

"That's ridiculous, Jake! Where'd you come up with such a crazy idea?"

But Jake was barely listening. He stood up and started pacing around the kitchen, figuring it out.

"It makes perfect sense! The story is a hundred years old. The McGregor family has lived on this farm for over a hundred years, so the timing is right. Maybe you didn't know exactly *where* the giant hand skeleton was buried in the field, Grandpa. Maybe you even thought it was just a story too, but I bet you always wondered if it was true. Now you know. We found the tip of one of the bones when we dug the post hole for the shed! You were surprised at what I found at the bottom of the post hole. *That's* why you filled it in!"

Jake was breaking into a sweat.

"It explains the FLIES! You disturbed them when you laid out the shape of the shed with stakes. They came up out of the ground!"

"Sit down, Jake," his grandfather said quietly. "Calm down. You'll get yourself all worked up again. A giant hand, son? Where would it have come from? Really? I mean, just think about that."

Jake was breathing hard, trying to catch his breath.

"But the giant flies, Grandpa! The white stone at the bottom of the hole...." Jake didn't want to stop, now that his grandpa was at least *listening* to him.

"Maybe those were cicadas, Jake. It's cicada season. They have been known to swarm. And the white ... stuff ... *if* it exists, maybe it's chalk."

"No. Not cicadas, not chalk! You know it, and I know it. They were FLIES! They've been chasing me for days. And it's BONE!"

Jake was getting upset now. He could feel himself close to tears. He started shouting.

"Why won't you tell me the truth, Grandpa? I know bone when I see it! The Cuthberts have a moose skull outside their new cabin. The bone at the bottom of the hole is just like it — white and grainy and strong!"

Jake's eyes were wild and he was leaning on the kitchen table, nose-to-nose with his grandfather. Gus was up on his feet, ready to bark.

His grandpa sighed and pushed away his dinner plate. "Sit down, Jake. Calm down, for heaven's sake. It's true this farm has been in our family for over one hundred years. Strange stories get told and passed down, but you should remember this: they're *stories*. No one knows for sure if they happened or not. Like poor old Edwina Fingles wanders off and disappears, and suddenly she becomes the swamp creature. Or a huge old prehistoric tree, or ancient animal bones or something, turn up in a field and someone makes up a story about a giant hand. People have huge imaginations, Jake, especially bored people."

"But Grandpa, I went to the library. Mrs. Cody knew who I was. She was nice until I asked her about the giant hand, then I saw her take a clipping from the wall. I know I did. She probably wanted to protect you and hide the truth."

His grandpa stayed silent, so Jake went on.

"And ... and ... at the library, Kate and Chris and I found a picture of the farm with the hand. There was a *horse-head pump* in the background! It has to be here, Grandpa! THE GIANT HAND IS ON THIS FARM!"

Jake and his grandpa looked at each other for a long time. Jake could hear his heart beating, could hear the farmhouse kitchen clock ticking on the wall ... heard a fly buzzing somewhere nearby ... time stood still.

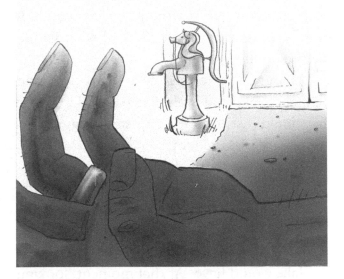

Anything could happen next. Truth or fiction, lies or tall tales, Jake was sure his grandpa was about to tell him something that would change everything.

He waited. And waited. Finally, his grandfather sighed and rubbed his chin. He looked up at Jake. When he spoke, he suddenly sounded to his grandson like an old, old man.

"I didn't know about the horse-head pump in the picture." Jake's grandpa hesitated, then went on, slowly. "I always hoped that one day this farm would be yours, Jake.

I don't know about a giant hand. I've heard the stories, yes. I've wondered. There's no way to know the truth, not for sure. Not unless we dug up the field. And what would be the point?"

His grandpa looked so old, so tired and sad, that Jake suddenly felt bad. Like maybe he should just forget it and stop bugging his grandpa about the truth.

Maybe the truth didn't really matter after all. The story was as good as the truth would ever be or maybe better. If it hurt people to get to the truth, maybe he should just leave it alone.

Jake would have. At that moment, looking at his tired old grandpa, he would have let it be right then and there. But his grandpa went on quietly, like something needed to be said and now no one could stop him.

"But there *is* something you should know, Jake. You may not like it." His grandpa paused and sighed like he was carrying a heavy weight on his shoulders.

He continued. "Just remember, there are different kinds of stories. Some are true, some are lies, and some are in-between. You have to decide for yourself what's true ... and what isn't. And for what it's worth, I'm not sure what I believe myself."

He got up and walked slowly to a table in the hallway.

He looks so old! Jake thought sadly. He watched his grandpa yank open a drawer and pull out a huge old key. He shoved the key across the table at Jake.

"Here. The fourth cold room on the left," his grandpa said. "And I hope you'll forgive me," he whispered.

Then the old man turned his back. Jake wasn't entirely sure, but he thought before he turned away, his grandpa's eyes shone with tears.

CHAPTER 18

PROOF IN HAND

Jake watched his grandpa shuffle away. He hesitated, but just for a second.

What's down there? Do I want to know? ... YES!

He snatched the key from the table then ran down the farmhouse stairs two at a time. He snapped on the light at the bottom of the stairs and the bulb slowly buzzed to life. He breathed in the musty, cobwebby smell of the place.

One, two, three, four doors.

Jake stood in front of the fourth cold room on the left.

It was locked. He fit the old key into the padlock and the door swung open with a huge *creak*.

It even sounds spooky!

The cold room was ... cold. And dark. And it smelled like decay and leaves and dirt. And something else. Time maybe. Or something forgotten. He flicked the light switch and the bulb slowly flickered to life.

The shelves were empty. The dirt floor was cold and damp. It took a moment for Jake's eyes to adjust to the dim light ...

... something gleamed out of the dark. Something dull and *yellow*. Jake gasped.

A golden circle was leaning up against the wall of the cold room. It filled the room from floor to ceiling. The circle was taller than Jake's head and wider than his arms spread out.

It was a huge, heavy golden circle. It practically took up the entire room.

Jake ran his hand over the cool, gleaming metal. It was perfectly smooth and made a circle that reached the dark ends of the cold room. His hand caught at something rough on the inside of the circle. He pushed his face closer to the metal and saw a letter stamped on the inside. It was a giant "T." Jake looked closer; it was hard to see in the gloom. There was another letter beside it: "O."

There were more letters, all around the inside of the circle. Jake ran his hands over the circle and whispered the letters to himself as he read them: "T-O-M-L-O-V-E-L-O-N-O-U-R-W-E-D-D-I-N-G-D-A-Y."

Jake froze. He realized it was a sentence: "*To M Love L on Our Wedding Day.*"

A chill started in Jake's feet and rose over his whole body, right to the top of his head. He didn't want to say the words on his lips, but he couldn't stop them:

"It's not a gold *CIRCLE!* It's a gold *RING!* It's a golden wedding ring big enough for a ... *GIANT.*"

And it came from a giant's rotting hand!

A scream started in Jake's throat. He tore back up the stairs and out the kitchen door. He ran down the lane, screaming, waving his arms wildly, and he never looked back.

He couldn't. A swarm of giant flies chased him, buzzing like chainsaws all the way.

THIS PART IS ALSO (MOSTLY) TRUE ...

Welcome to the end of the story, and if you've made it this far, congratulations. I told you at the beginning that it was scary and more than a little sad, and yet here you are. I'm sure you'll never look at a farmer's field again without wondering what secrets, and possibly what horrors, lie beneath it.

You've no doubt got many questions at this point. You're probably wondering what happened next, what happened to Jake, and you might be thinking ... is this story *true*?

It certainly seems true, doesn't it? But if you remember on the very first pages of this story you read these words: *Truth is an odd thing; one person's truth can be another person's lie. That's the most important thing to remember about this story: sometimes things that seem like lies are actually true. And sometimes you never can tell.*

I could leave the story right there, and you'd just have to accept it, wouldn't you?

But that would be unfair of me and I pride myself on being fair. So, without further ado, here are the answers you seek....

It was a *long* time before Jake went back to his grandpa's farm (he skipped a few summers), although he did eventually visit again. Once he did go back, he and his grandpa never discussed the giant hand, not ever. He loved his grandpa too much not to visit, and they managed to enjoy each other's company once again. There were just some things they didn't talk about. They never did build a shed, either.

On the plus side, Grandpa stopped telling crazy stories, lies, exaggerations, or whatever else you want to call them, which was a good thing as far as Jake was concerned.

He visited Kate and Chris Cuthbert again, since they were great friends. But *no one* was allowed to tell ghost stories. Ever. Chris was fine with that, and more surprisingly, so was Kate. They spent lots of time in the ginger-bread cabin in the woods, playing cards and making s'mores and *not* telling stories. At Jake's request, they kept a can of extra-strength bug spray under the cabin sink.

Jake also stayed away from the library for a while, although he was always polite to Mrs. Cody whenever he saw her on the street. She was polite too, but Jake knew better than to ask her about the giant hand. Or about anything else, for that matter.

See, Jake *had* figured out the truth about the giant hand. He wished with all his heart that he hadn't, that he'd left well enough alone and not pushed his grandpa to tell him what was down there, under the secret soil of the green field. He wished he could un-know the truth about the fourth cold room on the left, too.

But truth is a funny thing. Once learned, there is no way to unlearn it, short of amnesia.

So for Jake, there was no going back, no way to forget the truth about the hideous, dismembered, unmentionable THING buried deep in his grandpa's field. The giant white hand that really was somehow lying there beneath the field, a horrible truth hidden in the dark.

You're probably wondering, what happened to the bizarre giant gold wedding ring hidden in the farmhouse basement? That I can't answer, not for sure (see how unreliable I am!). Although I can tell you that Jake eventually had all the cold rooms removed and the damp old basement renovated and updated to be brightly lit, clean, and pleasant.

Jake inherited the farm, you see, and times being hard and jobs not easy to come by, he moved in when his grandfather died many years later. It was a beautiful farm, after all, and Jake McGregor became a successful farmer. He married a lovely girl (no one you know) and had a big family with six children. Jake was a great farmer and a wonderful father and husband.

There was a strange story circulating for a while about him digging madly in the back field one night. Someone said they saw him and his eldest son rolling a giant golden circle into the field by moonlight. Then they buried it. These are the same people who will tell you that they saw him from time to time, digging back there, particularly when times were tough and money was scarce. They'd see him in the moonlight, raising a shovel or turning an auger after a poor harvest, for instance.

But no one had any proof, so I can't tell you if that part of the story is true or not. It *is* true that Jake McGregor was always a wealthy man. When other farmers struggled, he always seemed to have gold in abundance, which he took to the bank in exchange for cash. His family was always well fed and well dressed, and once a year he made a modest donation to local shelters, children's groups, and the library always got a little something, too.

Make of that what you will. There are some secrets that even I can't answer. I can't tell you absolutely everything, now can I? What would be the fun in that?

So now you know the story of Jake McGregor and the giant hand. Despite the horrible truth, he grew up wealthy, happy, and wise.

There were only two things that were a little odd about Jake.

One: He always carried a golden fly swatter with him, everywhere he went (even though the giant flies that plagued the farm for years when he was younger were long gone).

Two: He would sometimes stop you in the middle of a conversation and ask with a crazy look on his face, "Do you hear a BUZZZZ?"

THE GARGOYLE AT THE GATES

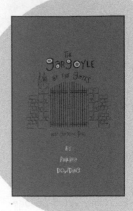

Christopher is astonished to discover that gargoyles Ambergine and Gargoth are living in the park next door and that Katherine, a girl from his class, knows the gargoyles, as well. When the Collector steals Ambergine, it's up to Christopher and Katherine to get her back, as long as something else doesn't catch them along the way.

Shortlisted for the Hackmatack Children's Choice Book Award, the 2013 Diamond Willow Award, and commended for the 2013 White Raven Award.

• •

"This lively, fast-paced novel by Philippa Dowding moves fluidly from the whimsical to the fantastical and takes an intriguing detour to some dark places in between."
—Quill & Quire

THE STRANGE GIFT OF GWENDOLYN GOLDEN

Gwendolyn Golden has a bad temper and hates to read. She's a pretty normal teenager until ... one morning she wakes up on the ceiling. Along with her many average teenage qualities, Gwendolyn Golden can also fly. What's happening to her?

• •

VISIT PHILIPPA DOWDING AT
www.pdowding.com

 @phdowding   f /philippa.dowding

Available at your favourite bookseller.

⛪ DUNDURN

VISIT US AT
Dundurn.com
@dundurnpress
Facebook.com/dundurnpress
Pinterest.com/dundurnpress